"*How to Order the Universe* is a dreamscape of a book. In an assured and striking voice, María José Ferrada tells the story of M, a girl who skips school to join her traveling salesman father on the road. Along the way, M witnesses tragedy, desire, secrecy, and grief as she finds her own truths and learns to separate her father's disappointments from her own. I adored this compelling, wise, and utterly unique coming-of-age tale."

—TARA CONKLIN, author of *The Last Romantics*

"Ferrada's novel has the poetic simplicity and dark wisdom of a fairytale. In it, we experience the machinations of repression during Chile's dictatorship through the eyes of a seven-year-old girl and, at the same time, through the adult version of this girl, who bears the burden of memory. Over the course of the story, both girl and woman attempt to understand the transience of existence and human connection. Ferrada gifts us with a story that is like an egg: complex in its simplicity, and full of life and mystery. I wanted to hold it close, and with great care."

—FRANCES DE PONTES PEEBLES,
author of *The Air You Breathe*

HOW TO ORDER THE UNIVERSE

Published by Tin House, Portland, Oregon

Distributed by W. W. Norton & Company

Library of Congress Cataloging-in-Publication Data

Names: Ferrada, María José, 1977- author. | Bryer, Elizabeth, 1986-
    translator.
Title: How to order the universe : a novel / María José Ferrada ;
    translated by Elizabeth Bryer.
Other titles: Kramp. English
Description: Portland, Oregon : Tin House, [2021] | Originally published in
    Spanish as 'Kramp'.
Identifiers: LCCN 2020037761 | ISBN 9781951142308 (hardcover) | ISBN
    9781951142315 (ebook)
Classification: LCC PQ8098.416.E77 K7313 2021 | DDC 863/.7--dc23
LC record available at https://lccn.loc.gov/2020037761

First US Edition 2021
Printed in the USA
Interior design by Diane Chonette
www.tinhouse.com
Cover image: © AlexRoz / Shutterstock

How to Order the Universe

a novel

María José Ferrada

TRANSLATED BY ELIZABETH BRYER

 TIN HOUSE / Portland, Oregon

For D.

"You still owe me two hundred dollars."

Addie to her father, in *Paper Moon*

I

D began his career selling hardware items: nails, saws, hammers, handles, and door viewers, brand name Kramp.

The first time he left the guesthouse where he lived, with a sample case in hand, he couldn't work up the courage to step inside the city's leading hardware store—and this was back when the city was just a town—until he'd walked past it thirty-eight times.

His first sales attempt happened the same day a man took a step on the moon. The townspeople assembled in the square to watch the moon landing thanks to a projector the mayor had wheeled out to his office balcony, which cast the moving image onto a white sheet. Since it played no sound, the fire brigade band provided the backing track.

When D saw Neil Armstrong take his first step on the moon, he thought that anything was possible—all it took was the right attitude and the right outfit.

So, the next day, after approaching the hardware store for the thirty-ninth time, he stepped inside it, in the most polished shoes the city had ever seen, and offered his Kramp products to the person in charge. Nails, saws, hammers, handles, and door viewers. He didn't close a sale, but he was told to come back the following week.

D treated himself to a coffee and jotted down on the napkin: "Every life has its own moon landing."

Later, when D told his father that man had reached the moon, his father said it was an out-

and-out hoax, that God had created man with his *Humor*
feet on the ground and with no wings to speak of,
and everything else was lies spouted by the presi-
dent of the United States.

Either way, the following week D made his
own small step for mankind: he sold a half-dozen *Small and*
saws and a dozen door viewers. When he left the *big victories*
hardware store with the order inside his suitcase,
he felt that all moments of happiness, large and
small, deserved to be projected into a town square.

II

Over the next few weeks, D delivered three photographs and four Chilean escudos to the Traveling Salesmen Registry. Fifteen days later his ID was ready, no. 13709.

With the ID in his pocket, and at a discount that was equivalent to a commission for 2,356 saws, 10,567 nails, 3,456 hammers, or 1,534 door viewers, he bought a Renault. Seated inside it, he started making trips to nearby towns, following the advice of an old-timer salesman. Really it was a piece of advice and a declaration.

The piece of advice:

"When you come to a town, your first task is to find the central coffeehouse and the hotel where the other traveling salesmen stay. Usually it's on the same block as the town square and the bar."

(That's where he would come across the men who, from that moment forward, would be a kind of floating family. A family with no relatives and, for that reason, more tolerable than any other.

The Made-in-China plastic-products salesman.

The Parker Pen salesman.

The English cologne salesman.

And everybody else.)

The declaration:

"All towns are the same: godforsaken shit heaps."

It is their nature, and there is nothing you can do to change the nature of things.

III

Bit by bit, D started to construct his own epistemology. And the first thing he did was separate life events into two groups: the probable and the improbable.

It was probable that he would visit seventeen clients that week. It was probable that ten of them would make a purchase. And it was probable that it would rain, because it was winter.

It was improbable, and D repeated this as he looked at himself in the mirror, that a house constructed from 80 percent Kramp products would collapse in the event of an earthquake or a tornado.

And it was improbable that, due to a bus workers' strike, a woman would be hitchhiking to university on the very same corner that D's Renault passed.

That was exactly what happened on 13 November 1973.

D thought she was the most beautiful woman in the world. And the woman, who hadn't laughed for a long time, thought D was talkative and entertaining.

A year later, on 13 November 1974, they got married.

On leaving the Civil Registry, D asked the woman to wait a second and went to find a serviette, where he jotted down what had just happened (their wedding) in a subcategory of his classification of things that he baptized "truly improbable things" ("those phenomena that make us think that some kind of god exists").

D seems almost child-like

IV

D and the beautiful woman built a house out
of Kramp products and, some time later, had a
daughter they called *M*. I am M.

Soon, my parents designed a learning plan that
would allow me to comprehend the things that
a child—a girl, in this case—needed in order to
make her way in the world.

Thus, I began early with a classification of things.

In my first year of life I discovered, for example,
that there is something called *day* and something
called *night*, and that everything that happens in
life fits into one of those two categories.

The second year I learned to look out the window. My parents told me that, over the course of my life, I would win and lose many things. I shouldn't worry; the world would still be out there.

The third year I discovered the existence of people. Once more, my parents used the window to explain to me that people could be classified as either summer people or winter people. I still don't know what they meant by that.

In my fourth year of life, I stepped out onto the patio of my house and saw fireflies. I decided that this would be my very own, unclassifiable memory. Fireflies that never stopped glowing.

V

When I was seven (it was a spring day, I know so because my mind insists on drenching that memory in a yellow hue), I heard the story of the moon landing and its moral for the first time: with well-shined shoes and the right outfit, anything is possible. And, to shield me from the nature of life, I think, D added that a little luck was needed too.

The same afternoon I polished my patent leather shoes with a brush, put on a green dress that I teamed with green socks, and decided I would be D's assistant.

I went out to the patio, lit a cigarette, and took a slow drag. I'd stolen it from D's pack, for in the evenings he fell asleep smoking in front of the television.

VI

I'd inherited from D an uncommon gift for persistence. So, a week later we got into the Renault—which now had, on both its doors, a Kramp products logo—and we set out for a neighboring town.

When we arrived and parked the car by the town square, D gave me a few instructions:

1. Smile.
2. Go for a walk if you get bored, but don't venture beyond the same block.
3. Say *thank you* if the person in charge gives you a chocolate or anything.

And he promised that if we closed a sale or collected the amount owing for the previous month's sale, in the late afternoon we would go to the coffeehouse.

We visited three stores that sold Kramp products alongside chocolates, toys, buttons, magazines, colognes, and dishcloths. On our first few trips, I could already see that objects designed for a vast array of uses established a sort of camaraderie in the town stores. I developed the habit of searching the display cabinets for objects with no apparent relationship to each other and telling myself that, if I discovered whatever the relationship was, I would have a lucky day (a wooden pencil was connected to a metal handle because the handle would be put on a door one day. A wooden door. Pencil–wood, wood–door. Luck).

That afternoon we sold three hundred saws and collected two amounts owing for sales closed the previous month.

I was also given a puzzle book and a can of pineapple, for which I said thank you.

In the late afternoon we went to the coffee-house. So began our partnership.

Simple cause and effect narration

VII

Everything that happened next was only possible because my mother was absent. It wasn't that she left the house much, it was that a part of her had abandoned her body and now resisted coming back.

Maybe that fragment of my mother was an astronaut, and on one of her journeys through outer space she had come across D (who since the moon landing had developed the habit of peering at the sky every so often) and had decided that the part of her that did come back would stay with him. Or, rather, with us.

But touchdowns are never easy and, during hers, my mother lost half the vision in her left eye.

In that blind spot, what I referred to as my double life started to take place.

A mother who was whole would have noticed. Did that make my mother irresponsible?

I don't think so; I think that, instead, life had been a bit irresponsible with her.

VIII

I started to think of our excursions, which usually lasted an entire day, as a practical subject—<u>an extension of my schooling</u>.

D and my mother had come to an agreement: I could be his assistant only after school and during vacations. And no matter what day it was, I had to be home by nine.

But deals never meant much to D, or to my mother, so most days we kept on past the school gate and headed for the highway.

After hearing so much talk about Kramp products, I started using them as a way to comprehend the workings of the world, and that was how, while my classmates wrote poems about trees and the summer sun, I wrote odes to door viewers, pliers, and saws.

I also invented instruments such as the "Adding Machine," which was a rectangular piece of chipboard equipped with nails and nuts (it was a regular abacus, but I called it that, the "Adding Machine").

I remember how, at school camp, when we were out looking at the stars, I used the Southern Cross as a reference point and explained to my classmates that the specks that shone so brightly in the distance weren't stars but three-inch tacks that the Great Carpenter had used to hang the whole sky. Us included.

What I'm trying to say is that every person tries to explain the inner workings of things with whatever is at hand. I, at seven years of age, had reached out my hand, and had grasped a Kramp catalogue.

IX

HARDWARE STORES

Every construction is the sum of its parts, parts that are joined by fittings.

D explained it like this: a building, even the biggest in the world, relies upon a structure held together by bolts. Which was the equivalent of saying:

1. The big and the small complement each other.
2. Just one bolt, if poorly fitted, can bring about the end of the world. And the building, as it toppled, would tear

down another, and that other building, in a terrible domino effect, would do the same to the neighboring building, on and on until the whole city, entire countries, even civilization itself, was razed to the ground.

The workings of ecosystems, the law of cause and effect, relativity—"every subject matter can be understood by looking inside a box of hardware," D once said. "Same goes for the saws and hammers hanging from the wall."

EVERYBODY ELSE

As the old-timer salesman had predicted, the coffeehouse and the bar (I didn't visit the latter) together formed the center of the universe around which the planet of sales revolved. Nobody arranged to meet. It was simply known that everybody would be there at certain times of the day, hating on their goddamned luck.

The coffeehouses were private suns and, had anyone looked beneath the table, they would have seen an assortment of black shoes, painstakingly polished; sample cases; and a single pair of white shoes swinging from the chair—mine.

I liked breathing in the smoke from their cigarettes. Watching the salesmen order one coffee after another.

Listening to their lies, time and again.

C's STORY

C caused a woman to die from a heart attack when he sent her a truckload of a million needles. Only one thousand people lived in that town, so on seeing the truck pull up outside her store and the driver begin to unload the goods, the woman simply stopped breathing.

Truth be told, the orders were never exact. They had the habit of inflating. If somebody ordered a dozen of whatever, most likely a little more of the whatever would arrive. Imprecision (as well as going to great pains to avoid signing any kind of documentation—in this case, the order) was one of the first laws of sales, and of life.

The story about the needles had happened a long time ago, but it was repeated until we were dead tired of it.

The first time I heard it I felt sorry for the woman but, soon after, a smile escaped me, and then a chuckle, to which I added a clap, which merged with the smoke and the chuckles of everybody else.

F's STORY

F's is a simple story. He came to a certain town, and there he finished off a barrel of rum.

Every salesman has their "story"

F then hopped aboard the train, took a nap, and, when he woke, found himself in the same town he'd left. It was the same time of day, but the calendar was showing the next day's date. On top of losing a day of his life, F had lost both his sample case and his suitcase.

Every time he told the story he was asked if he'd paid for a return fare. And then the person posing the question would erupt into noisy laughter.

I liked to imagine that circular trip: a train with F inside it, traveling ad infinitum around a planet in the shape of a barrel.

S's STORY

One afternoon, S left a godforsaken town (he always said that: *godforsaken town*) and crashed his Citroneta into the side of a bridge. As can be expected, the guardrail gave way, and S plunged into the river. The impact was so powerful that the Citroneta broke into a thousand pieces, and S was knocked unconscious; he drifted down the river atop one of the car doors.

Hours or maybe days went by until he ran aground on the bank of another town, "which, as well as godforsaken, was very poor." The locals took S, who was still unconscious, and who over the course of his ordeal had lost all his clothing, to a house where they tried to revive him. When they met with no luck, they dressed him in the clothes of a scarecrow and took him to the only hospital, where, weeks later, he regained consciousness.

When he arrived at his house ten kilos lighter and dressed as a scarecrow, his dog didn't recognize him, and he discovered his third wife had run off with a pharmacist. "Because one calamity is always followed by another," rounded off S, who was my favorite.

HOW TO ORDER THE UNIVERSE

The story varied each time S told it. The door that had saved him from sure death was sometimes a wheel or a tree trunk that had happened to float down the river. The scarecrow's clothing could be a curtain, the clothes of a dead man, or somebody's quilt.

Through lies, tell the truth

X

Days went by, and into D's sample case I slipped letters of this kind:

"I like being your assistant."

And in lieu of a signature I drew flowers and "lucky beetles."

D responded to the letters with phrases like:

"I'm pleased!"

And in lieu of a signature he drew fish and whales.

XI

Sometimes another kind of relative joined the family of traveling salesmen: people seeking free travel.

Within this group, there were two classes: idealists who believed in the kindness of strangers, and stingy individuals who were prepared to talk for the whole trip to save what the fare would have cost.

I never managed to classify E as belonging to either category, so I decided to position him halfway between.

E's job was to screen films at the university cinema.

As well as screening them, he sourced them, and he was responsible for opening and closing the cinema too. His fifth duty consisted in charging a fee that most filmgoers didn't pay. This didn't bother E, as his aim wasn't to turn a profit (the business wasn't his), but to have others watch the film so he would have someone to talk to about it afterward.

And it was thanks to *2001: A Space Odyssey* that D and E met. D was not really a film buff, but sometimes he "needed" to see a film. That's how he explained it. Generally, the films he "needed" to see were about detectives or boxers. But that day, on seeing the image of the spaceship orbiting the moon, which is the opening of Kubrick's film, he had an epiphany: he, not the machine, was orbiting the earth. And, seen from above, the earth was a speck, a tack like all the others, lost in that great timber structure that was the dawn of time. Due to a distancing effect, everything was condemned to disappear. To disconnect. To keep hurtling head-long toward who knows where.

They watched the film three times in a row. That was the other advantage of E's cinema. If the viewers wanted to watch the film again, E could start it over. It wasn't for nothing that E was the operator; within that bastion of uncomfortable chairs, things were done his way.

After E closed the cinema for the day, they went to a bar. And, though it was always best not to talk about politics, they talked. And since they were on that topic, they touched on religion too.

On arriving at that place of trust and transcen-dence, D told E about Kramp products, and E told D that his true passion wasn't film but black-and-white photography.

When they were on their third bottle of wine, E said that there was a town that he wanted to photograph in particular, a ghost town, which was located on the route that D's Renault (which, when viewed from the moon, was a speck that looked like it had come to a standstill along a straight line) took every week.

XII

Before long, D and I had something like a modus operandi in place.

When we came to a town, before stepping inside any hardware store, we verified that our shoes were shiny—in the case of the contrary, D had a brush in the glove box—and lit a cigarette. A lucky cigarette.

The latter was a right I gained in the third or fourth month, once D had confirmed the value of my presence beside him whenever he approached a counter.

"Your mother can't know about this."

"Of course not," I said, letting out a tiny puff of smoke.

We headed for the hardware stores, and the scene was the same in all the towns, with three possible variants: things were good, things were so-so, or things were bad. It all depended on how Kramp products had performed since our last visit.

1. Products delivered and sold without a hitch: things were good (in such cases, usually D collected the amount owing and sold something else, and I was given a cheap gift).

2. Products delivered but not sold: things were so-so. When this happened, D uttered some adage about time: it's all a matter of time, put on a brave face in bad times, give it time. And we hurried out.

3. Products delivered but with varia-
    tions: things were bad. This meant
    that there were discrepancies between
    what the person in charge had ordered
    and what had arrived, usually intro-
    duced intentionally by D. And there
    were times when the company offered
    special incentives to sell one product
    or another: May, month of nuts; June,
    month of hammers; July, month of
    Phillips-head screwdrivers. In these
    cases, the affected party's reaction
    depended on the number of times it
    had happened and the nature of the
    product, for receiving an oversupply
    of two thousand umbrellas at the
    beginning of winter wasn't the same
    as receiving the same consignment at
    the beginning of summer.

This final scenario was where, most of the time, my work began. Because it was one thing to tell a man clutching a sample case that he was shameless, and quite another to tell him so when his other hand was clutching mine.

And I didn't speak, only fixed my gaze on the person in charge.

In another life, I had learned different kinds of gazes: an indifferent gaze, a sweet gaze with a touch of melancholy, a bored-and-desperate gaze. The final resort was my on-the-brink-of-tears gaze. And that was the most intense of all. If the person in charge focused on my pupils, instead of encountering me, he or she encountered every possible form of fragility: world hunger; ice sculptures that, after so much effort, were reduced to water; the Soviet space-dog Laika turning around and around and around in the long night of infinity. All things had come to inhabit those small dark circles. Because that was the nature of life: to be small and dark. *You know it, D knows it, in my seven short years I know it, and you, what do you do? You insult it because of an oversupply of nails and nuts. End it already, end this nonsense, end all this.*

I thought this but didn't say it, for I was aware that a single word could break the tension and dramatic effect that I'd learned to wield in a few short months.

We came and went along the highways. And when we'd done so for around one year—roughly the halfway point of my career—I asked D for a commission commensurate with my talent. It was only fair, considering that I worked hard every day, whether by practicing in front of the mirror or by experimenting with my school friends using the same silent method—retracting my friendship, and then extending it again in exchange for a sandwich or magazine.

Before going on I should clarify that my motivation wasn't only material. It was also an early bid to discover the weaknesses of the human heart, a search for justice.

Thinking about what I'd learned in my math class, I continued:

"I want my share, one-tenth."

"Forget it."

I wasn't exactly sure how to keep dividing, so I responded:

"In that case I want seven pesos for every hundred that you take in."

"Forget it."

"Five pesos for every hundred or I won't come with you ever again."

I remember that we were in a coffeehouse, and D lifted his gaze from the yellow cards on which he was making a note of the orders and looked at me, sizing up how genuine my words were and making a quick mental review of the status attributed to childhood around the world. Accepting my deal would make him the employer of a child, and child labor had been forbidden for a while now. But there was also Einstein, who had said that thing about everything being relative. We hadn't understood him, but some element of his declaration had stayed with us.

I couldn't go home with money in my pocket because it would come to my mother's attention, and, if she took up the thread and started pulling, she would find out about my truancy and D's irresponsibility.

I couldn't go home with money, but:

"We'll do a quid pro quo."

"And what's that."

"I won't give you money, but each time we make a sale of more than one hundred thousand pesos, I'll buy you something."

"I accept."

During the trip that followed my negotiation, we closed a sale for a special offer on drill bits. Beautiful drill bits, many, very many drill bits, drill bits to fill an entire town, the entire world—and even, it seemed to me, an entire galaxy.

The first thing I wanted was a sample case the same as D's, but yellow. I'd seen it in a toy shop.

When we went to look for it, the yellow sample case was no longer there, but as a consolation D bought me a nurse's carrying case. A plastic one, with a white cross in the middle, which I started to use each time I went to work with D, making the part I was playing more realistic.

Soon, to the carry case was added an array of dolls, each dressed in their country's traditional clothing; a green coat with a brooch; a yellow Mickey Mouse thermos; a reversible cap; a puffer vest; and a dozen other things that I jotted down on the notepad I always carried with me, under the title reimbursements.

Approaching eight years of age, I had discovered that, while D was nothing special as a father, he made an excellent employer.

XIII

A week after seeing the continuous showing of *2001: A Space Odyssey*, D dropped by the cinema again.

And he said to E:

"That town you wanted to visit isn't in the category of conquered territories, or in the category of territories yet to be conquered, but I can take you tomorrow."

"What do you mean?"

"It doesn't have a hardware store."

"And so?"

"Don't you worry. I'll be out the front tooting the horn at ten on the dot."

María José Ferrada

In hindsight, D was the one who should have been worried. But since he wasn't, at ten on the dot he went by E's, and he deposited him in the main square of the ghost town, which he would do many times over the next few months.

While E took his photographs and made his enquiries, D would go to the neighboring town to fill it with locks and nuts. When he was done, he would return to the ghost town to collect E.

On the way back, they spoke about all sorts of topics, and, among other things, E told D that a foreign newspaper was interested in his photographs.

For D, anywhere abroad was excessively far away, so they changed the subject and spoke about the film that would screen at the cinema the next week: *To Kill a Mockingbird*, starring Gregory Peck.

XIV

Sales, like any form of work, was a means of survival. And as with most other means of survival, the average human being couldn't make it to the end of the month, but only approximately to day fifteen. From then on, the human being was obliged to fall back on his friends, on cheques with thirty-day clearances, on pawnshops, and on moneylenders, the latter only in extreme cases. It happened to everybody, D included.

Smaller-scale strategies were added to the general ones and, all told, served the overall objective to survive.

These ploys were carried out every day and had slight variations, depending on the trade. In the case of sales, they functioned roughly like so:

INVOICES

This strategy was viable in coffeehouses, restaurants, and even hotels. In the final two was where it really paid off. It was very simple: in the invoice description, you changed one coffee to two, one lunch to two, one night's stay to two. The company paid your expenses and, without knowing it, your partner's as well.

Because the complicity of all parties was required, generally this was only done in the coffeehouses, restaurants, and hotels that were frequented by traveling salesmen.

Some refined these strategies. I remember a hotel that also ran a clothing store. Sweaters, overcoats, boots, shirts, and ties were sweetly camouflaged under the concept of three nights' stay, when really it had been one.

We left the hotel warm and triumphant. This wasn't theft; it was tiny spoils from the war that all human beings must unleash against the system that oppresses them. So thought the intellectuals who, from a coffeehouse, had observed the world's workers. We, in another coffeehouse, hadn't thought it, but we knew it in the bottom of our just-as-tiny hearts. This wasn't theft. And even if it had been, we wouldn't have cared.

ROAD TOLLS

The Reimbursement of Expenses Strategy had a fundamental problem: you had to account for the expenses.

Every week D had to send off a spreadsheet detailing invoices from hotels, restaurants, and—this was the most complex point—road tolls.

While there existed a circuit of hotels and restaurants that were prepared to falsify invoices, turning a road concession system to our advantage was simply beyond all possibility.

What we did, if we wanted to justify a trip we hadn't taken, was simple: the next time we passed by the toll booth, we parked the car on the highway verge and searched for the receipts that had been tossed out the window by people who traveled without accounting for their expenses.

The procedure was carried out judiciously. No more than one or two days could pass between the road toll you wanted to claim and the day you searched for it, because, after that point, the receipts would blow a long way down the highway, or they would be in poor condition due to the summer sun or winter rain.

Likewise, it wasn't worth getting too close to the road. We searched for the scraps of paper on the verge only, otherwise you ran the risk of getting hit by a car. And if that happened, it would be impossible to explain to my mother what I'd been doing hunting for scraps of paper on the side of the road on a school day. She was an absent mother, but that didn't mean we should abuse the fact.

No doubt she wouldn't have understood the quid pro quo or the parallel education system because, as D said, my mother was a sensitive woman, or the closest thing to sensitive we'd ever known. My mother was beautiful, and goodness and beauty were one and the same. "Scholastic philosophy said so, and last week's *Selections from Reader's Digest* did too," D continued. But I'd stopped paying attention.

XV

The day I met E—the photographer—he got into the passenger seat. I remember him saying something about the rows of poplars along the trails that led from the highway, and that a good black-and-white photograph was one that showed the whole spectrum of greys between each extreme. The light made the objects appear, or it made them disappear.

The light.

He made us pull over, and got out to photograph the poplars because E, unlike us, seemed to have all the time in the world.

D and I made the most of the interlude and lit a cigarette. E was one of those people whose very presence gives others permission to act naturally. The sort of person who doesn't expect you to arrive on time or, when you do arrive at last, to say something important. The sort of person who distrusts order and who, consequently, brings a little bit of chaos with him wherever he goes.

When finally he had photographed the trees, E showed me his photographic camera. It was a Canon FTb, the same model that reporters used to document the war in Vietnam.

The light, which made objects appear, or made them disappear.

The trace.

That was what E wanted to capture.

"I hunt ghosts with this camera."

"And what are they like?"

"White, and covered in a sheet that has holes for them to peer through."

What E didn't know was that, a few months later, he would be one too. In those years, our cities were full of them.

E knew this; E was searching for them; E summoned them. And, later, he would join his family.

That day, I remember we dropped him in the town, and, in the afternoon, we collected him before going back to the city.

"Did you find many?"

"Many what?"

"Ghosts."

"No, no luck today."

"Next time."

"Let me see . . . actually, I think I might have just found one, look here." Click.

The photograph that E took of me, which he gave me on our next trip, is one of the few keepsakes I have from the period. I'm in the back seat of the Renault, smiling and opening my eyes wide.

A black-and-white photo, with the whole spectrum of greys between each extreme.

XVI

The salesmen's destinations were cities and, mostly, towns.

These functioned as base camps, the strategic hearts of which were the hotels. Once set up, the salesmen embarked upon—we embarked upon—forays to conquer the neighboring territories. We were colonizers, and we wanted to convert the savages to the religion of Kramp products, Parker Pens, English cologne, or Made-in-China plastic products.

The more virgin territories there were, the better it was for us: the towns spontaneously recovered their virginity every thirty days, a time period that roughly coincided with the spell between the salesmen's visits.

These forays were governed by stricter rules than our usual trips, and during my two years of work I only went on four or five, as I could only take part during school breaks. And an eight-year-old girl, as a rule, isn't allowed to stay anywhere overnight without a reasonable explanation.

What I could do was skip school—which I was doing more and more often—and go home acting as though nothing out of the ordinary had happened, thanks to the enlightenment D provided: "Most of the time, complex problems require surprisingly simple solutions."

So we made a false booklet of parent–teacher communications that D signed (truancy), which coexisted with the real booklet of parent–teacher communications that my mother signed (meeting requests, museum visits, a farm excursion).

Depending on the circumstance, I had to hand over one booklet or the other.

"You must never mix up the booklets."

"Of course not."

It wouldn't have made a difference. With thirty students in the class, it was almost impossible for the teacher to memorize the narrative thread of any one of our booklets. And as for my mother, she was a reserved woman. Although, now that I think of it, she wasn't reserved. She was simply sad, and her sadness meant she couldn't pay attention to details.

The mother has an unspoken presence

Each highway, town, and city had its place in my parallel education about the workings of things. While the central cosmogony was associated with Kramp products, D added new elements whenever my comprehension required it.

The relationship between time and space, for example.

"Do you remember my telling you R's story?"

"The one about the man who faked his own death?"

"No, the one about the man who worked for the local council and used an entire year's budget to construct a landing strip for small planes—on which, of course, no small plane ever landed."

"I remember. He planned the whole thing when he was a kid. His classmates testified, saying that back then he would spend all day making paper planes."

"That's the one. Now, think: if that had happened in a city, how long would everybody have been telling the story?"

"Weeks."

"And if it had happened in a town?"

"Months."

"And if it had happened in a small town?"

"Years."

"Exactly."

We continued the trip in silence, and after the Renault had progressed roughly a kilometer, I said to D that there was a fourth option:

"If the town were really really really small they'd be telling R's story forever."

D said, "Most likely," and half a kilometer later he added that physics had yet to discover an explanation for this particular phenomenon, because an explanation had not yet been found for why those kinds of towns existed in the first place.

We could add to the relationship between time and space the evolution of the species theory, the expansion of the universe theory, and even some basic notions of physics and theology.

My comprehension of the world expanded like a sponge, especially when you include everything I heard at the hardware store counters, in the coffeehouses, the hotels.

When, years later, I told my friends about these memories, I tried to make it clear that D hadn't been a fool—that's what my grandmother on my mother's side called him: "the fool"—but a pioneer of systemic pedagogy.

XVII

A couple of times, while D was collecting amounts owing, I accompanied E.

No, photographing ghosts certainly wasn't like photographing people.

It took a long time to find the ghosts. You had to ask questions, make calls from public telephone booths, and talk with people who were afraid of telling you what they knew.

"When a ghost withers, it becomes a bone.

And if it withers further, it becomes dust.

We have to find them before that stage," E explained to me.

María José Ferrada

And when he finished his sentence, for the
first time ever, I experienced a strange feeling that
I defined as a black-hole feeling.[1]

---

1 A sadness that, even though you feel it, doesn't
belong to you.

XVIII

The day that E—the photographer—met my mother, a strange silence descended.

It was the weekend, and E had come by our place to bring D an old film projector. But as much as they tried, they couldn't get it to work.

And so, to show that E hadn't made the trip in vain, D invited him to stay for lunch.

That was when my mother came in. She'd been pruning the magnolia in the garden.

When D introduced them, E and my mother looked at each other with familiarity. With sadness, too.

"We know each other," said my mother.

"We had a friend in common at university," added E.

From then on, everything was strange. Lunch was served, but E didn't talk about photographs or ghosts, and my mother, who always seemed to be on another planet, this time appeared to be striving to reach another galaxy.

I, accustomed to salvaging uncomfortable situations—there wasn't a huge difference between a hardware store counter and our family table—intuited that the only thing bringing us together in that moment, and therefore the thing that could save us, was the film we'd seen on television the day before. My mother and I had watched it, and D, who had arrived just as the film was ending, said he'd seen it too. E had seen many films, so I was confident he knew it too.

I started talking about *The Bridge on the River Kwai*.

Five minutes later we were all talking about *The Bridge on the River Kwai*.

D and E started talking about World War II and the Chinese (in my head at the time, the Japanese and the Chinese lived in one country), and we still had time to whistle the film's theme song.

That's what I was doing when, looking at the bowl of asparagus soup, I had an epiphany, the first in my life.

Steam was rising from the bowl, and it transformed into a ghost the size of my thumb. That first ghost was followed by a second, a third, a fourth ghost.

This procession of ghosts from the afterlife sprouted from the soup and moved above the table, trying to communicate with the beforelife. But they didn't manage to. Poor things.

When I mentioned my strange vision after coming out of my trance, my mother burst into tears and E said it was time to go.

D, who couldn't find any conceivable analogy in the Kramp catalogue to help him comprehend what was happening, told E no problem but to please leave him the film projector.

My mother shut herself in her room for the rest of the afternoon, and D and I stayed in the dining room.

"If we fix the projector, what should we watch?" I asked.

"A pirate film."

"Okay," I said, feigning an exaggerated enthusiasm and hugging D, an atypical expression of affection that neither of us was accustomed to.

Epiphanies were almost always followed by insight, as I would confirm over the years, and that day I realized the following:

D was alone.

I was alone.

Life was a lonely place.

And this fact belonged to the category of "Things that Were Simply the Way They Were."

So I left D tinkering with the projector and went to my room to read my comics.

XIX

In the town stores there was no disorder, only dynamic order. You didn't have to be especially smart to comprehend the true nature of town stores: they were proto-anarchic systems.

From the simple to the complex:

Stores where objects were grouped together according to their nature (umbrellas only, hats only, tobacco only).

Stores where objects were ordered according to spatial criteria (everything that fit between a pin and a lawnmower, from right to left).

Stores where objects grouped according to an as-yet undeciphered numerical sequence (counters that displayed seven forks, fifteen shirts, eighteen plastic buckets, and so on).

This final category was what most caught my attention, because I thought that discovering the sequence would bring me a little closer to comprehending the classifications used by the Great Carpenter to order the universe.

Whatever the case, the different shops illustrated the organizational possibilities that, through making associations, the human brain can concoct.

SHOE STORES

Out of all of them, my favorite was the shoe store that belonged to a German immigrant who had escaped a war and, as he fled, had observed the following:

1. The enemy is obliged to enter the battlefield through a space.
2. This space is bound by time.

Which was the equivalent of saying that if one manages to stop time, the enemy will be stopped in its tracks too.

Proud of his discovery, the German, whose father and grandfather were shoemakers, worked hard and saved enough money to continue the family business in this new land. After the grand opening, which the whole town attended—except for the greengrocer, an English immigrant who hated the Germans—he threw himself into accomplishing his central objective: to stall time.

The mechanism was simple: in his shoe store, he sold only shoes from the late forties—peacetime.

He'd bought many—so many that by the time his first load sold out, he'd trained several saddlers to make the shoes of the era.

Every time they visited the town, the traveling salesmen stopped by his store and asked for a pair of modern shoes, their sole purpose to hear the German roar and bellow about his opposition to war.

D and I went there occasionally.

And the day we sold a consignment of timber planers that had proved very tricky to move, we bought two pairs of shoes in celebration: black patent leather with wooden soles for me, and lace-up oxfords for D.

We slipped them on immediately, tossed our old ones in a dustbin by the door, and set out with shoes that could stop an enemy in its tracks.

SPECIAL STORES

There were special stores too. Stores that, considering the size of the towns, were big. The closest thing to a supermarket that the townspeople knew.

If you closed a sale in one of these stores, the consignment would occupy one whole freight wagon of the train. That's what they said. And, to fill it, the sale process would take a couple of days.

Not just one salesman made the trip, but several at the same time.

The Turk's store was famous. It was never about simply showing him the catalogues and samples. You also had to be capable of talking to the Turk for fifty-eight or seventy-two hours straight, pretty much. The salesmen slept overnight in rooms inside his house, which was a continuation of the shop. And the next morning, with hangovers that only the owner of the house awoke without, they took up where they had left off the night before.

The stories were prepared in the days leading up to the visit. For if the Turk had a good night, he bought huge quantities from everyone. If he didn't enjoy himself, he bought only what was necessary, which was more than enough all the same.

Not that it really mattered all that much, as, however long the marathon sale lasted, they ate and drank as if they had walked into a story from the *Thousand and One Nights*.

Only a select few were invited. Word got around the coffeehouses. Whoever went could consider himself a true salesman and, if the freight wagon was filled, a true hero of a war that was part pagan, part religious.

When, fifteen days later—the length of time it took for the order to be dispatched—the consignment passed along the railroad close to the highway, the salesmen tooted their horns.

It was a beautiful sound that only the chosen ones of sales heaven could understand.

XX

D had read in some magazine that thing about a happy worker being more productive and committed to the business. So, every now and then, instead of going to visit hardware stores, we would go to E's cinema, the university cinema. We would go in the mornings, not at the time it was open to the public (Monday to Thursday continuous showings from 4 p.m.; Wednesday cheap night), so the cinema was always empty.

I don't think D and E ever planned these visits. We went, and E was simply there. We got comfortable in the middle of the space, the lights went out, and it started: first the sound, and, seconds later, the film.

For as long as that form of remuneration for my early commitment to the trade lasted, we watched:

The Kid (twice).

Paper Moon (twice).

The Red Balloon (three times).

And a strange animated short film called *The Sand Castle* (once), which I never saw or heard mentioned again. Maybe I imagined it.

In any case, in all those films we cried, dried our tears, and noisily blew our noses, using two white, perfectly ironed handkerchiefs that D always carried in his pocket: one for him, the other for me.

Spurred by our taste for drama in dealing with the films—and with life—we asked for them to be replayed, using a method of my own invention that consisted of whistling and yelling, "Curtain turn!"

The phrase escaped all logic and grammar, but E understood that we wanted him to show the film again.

"No trouble at all. Quite the contrary; in times like these one appreciates an enthusiastic public," he would say.

It was when we stepped out after seeing *The Kid* for the second time that we spotted my mother at a distance.

She was in one of the university quadrangles with a group of people, who were all talking in a serious, disciplined way. I recognized her leather jacket and her backpack with its red star.

What was my mother doing there? My mother, who had left university years ago?

What was my mother talking about with that group of people?

Who were those people?

It was possible that my mother—who, when viewed from this far away, looked like one of my dolls—had also seen us and would add another question to the list:

What were we doing there, on a workday for D, and a school day for me?

After reaching that point, we would have three options:

One: Keep adding questions to the list: What were human beings doing on Planet Earth? What was the meaning of life?

Two: Talk to my mother and try to figure out an answer together. But an answer would have obliged us to give details about my parallel education, and my mother to tell us about her unknown friends.

The third option was to forget the whole thing. Maybe it wasn't my mother after all; maybe it was a woman who resembled my mother, someone who had my mother's tastes, someone who even wore the same clothes as my mother but was in fact someone else.

I vote for option three. I didn't say it, but I thought it.

I vote for option three. D didn't say it, but he thought it.

Fine, we agreed, in the room for silence that friendship allows. Because at this stage D was both my employer and one of those friends who understands that, most of the time, a good silence is more valuable than a good piece of advice.

So, we quickly crossed the university quadrangle, D with his black leather sample case, and I with my nurse's carry case.

On getting into the Renault we each lit a cigarette. And in recognition, I think, of the fact that I had grasped the complexities of human beings at such a young age, D showed me how to blow smoke rings.

María José Ferrada

Small rings that crossed the city, expanding
and dissolving in the distance.

XXI

Our sales model started to be analyzed across "the sector."

We were asked questions, and some salesmen even tried to convince their children to accompany them—with no success, thanks to insecure and overprotective mothers.

That was when S, that Moses of sales, had the idea to hire me. And it didn't seem such a bad idea.

He explained it like this: He and D sold different products: perfumery and hardware, respectively. I could accompany them on the same trip, changing my appearance ever so slightly. Nothing sophisticated, a simple hat would do it. He himself would buy it. Nobody would notice that in the morning I was daughter to one of them and, in the afternoon, daughter or niece to the other.

All that was needed was good timing and a little flexibility, this last requisite on my part.

Whatever S earned from the sales he closed in my company, he would give us a commission.

I listened to the plan with great interest, imagining the new hat and the commission. D paid me five pesos for every 100 earned in his quid pro quo system, but, taking into account the additional effort, as well as my growing clout before the store counters, I was sure that this time I could get ten out of every 100 in real money.

"Of course not," said D. And he thought of the samurai.

The logical thing would have been to call to mind feudal patriarchs, but maybe because he was still obsessed with fixing the film projector—brand-name

Fuji Photo Film—he thought of the samurai, and added:

"Under no circumstances."

In all ideals-based communities there is a code of honor, operating norms, "prin-ci-ples." And D always emphasized that last word, gave it a special cadence.

Then he launched into a speech about how violating a code of honor, so long as the code was effective, and independent of whether it was honorable, could cost the offender not only admonition from fellow community members but also, even worse, expulsion.

S and I looked at him in silence, not understanding where he was going with this.

"She can accompany you, but there'll be no money changing hands," D concluded.

I could have protested, but I knew that, in the sales society, I was not yet considered a true samurai, despite my strong performance. I was a tiny samurai, defending a tiny castle, capable of committing a tiny hara-kiri. Nothing more, but nothing less, either. The three of us were clear on that point and, for the moment, that should have been enough for my diminutive honor.

I maintained a stoic silence (with nothing but a light kick that I landed on an empty chair to give me away), but I couldn't help it when my angry gaze met S's happy one. It was at that point exactly that our gazes cancelled each other's out.

The thing is, deep down I felt something like affection toward S.

"When do we start?" I asked, forgetting the commission and remembering professionalism.

"Tomorrow," said S.

"I have a birthday party at school," I said.

"The day after tomorrow, then," said D.

"Okay," said S and I at the same time.

And we took that synchronicity as a sign that the deal was done.

XXII

The drives I most liked were the drives home. And it wasn't because home was at the end of the road, but because the late-afternoon light simplified everything. At that time of day, the world looked like a scale model I'd seen in one of the many hardware stores we visited.

Someone had cut out the trees and set them down along the straight line that out of convention we called a road, someone had whittled a house and put it there (had used steel shears and a gouge). And, following that logic, which the light prompted me to do, someone had fashioned us and put us here.

María José Ferrada

Great Carpenter, I whispered, as if aiming to irritate someone who was a little deaf.

XXIII

My double shift started, and the increase in my work hours was proportional to my absences from school.

D anticipated my teachers' potential concern and, to prevent them from calling my mother, invented a sickness for one of my grandmothers, the one on my mother's side. She was a second mother to me, we had a special bond (brand-name Kramp, 12 mm width), and I wanted to enjoy her last weeks on earth. He understood, and the school, the school understood too, of course. The relationship between grandparents and grandchildren was especially blessed by the Christian god, and my school was Catholic.

So, free from institutional pressures, I started to ply my trade with greater freedom.

Three days per week—the fake grandmother lived in another town—I skipped school and divided my time according to products: mornings, hardware; afternoons, perfumery and cosmetics.

I couldn't accompany D and S on long trips (we were still unable to find a way of justifying overnight stays to my mother when I wasn't on school break), but gaining the three days out of five away from school was a step almost as important as the one taken by astronauts.

PERFUMERY AND COSMETICS

Let's go see this thieving sonofabitch, S would say, before stepping inside each perfumery, a phrase that underwent a slight modification—

goddamned whore—if the manager or owner was a woman.

S repeated these words with such fervor every time he visited a client that, more than cursing, he seemed to be asking permission to start work from a god as foulmouthed as he. And the work consisted of selling shampoos, hand cream, nail polish and nail polish remover, eye shadows, and lipsticks.

S had his own way of meting out justice, which, in this case, meant adding an extra percentage to the prices the company gave him. *It didn't matter; the owners were Chinese morons who didn't check the invoices because these fucking Chinese didn't even know how to read.*

S explained everything in simple and direct terms. He had that virtue.

My modus operandi was roughly the same. I went into the stores with my well-shined shoes, plastic carry case, and the hat that S had bought me, and fixed my gaze on the person in charge.

There was something in the other's heart—the other being the person in charge—that I knew how to understand. A fine tapestry woven from mild aches and minor triumphs, where these existed—it was enough to look at the dusty street, at the counter—that stayed forever attached to their pupils. Few knew it. I was one of those few. And it was for that reason that I practiced my repertoire of gazes before the mirror, as these were my infallible instrument of connection.

I didn't close sales; what I did was practice sophisticated mental gymnastics.

And it worked. Because the ones in charge—those people—saw in me their own weakness and, after that, they let down their guard.

Meanwhile, S stopped being a simple sonofabitch—something in me still mimics S when I remember him, and still trusts in his foulmouthed god—to become a sonofabitch capable of feeling concern for "the daughter of his bedridden sister."

Invoices were being paid, and shampoos, hand cream, and nail polish remover were finding their places in the world.

S didn't have any qualms about disregarding the agreement and giving me a percentage of the sale in cash. One percent of earnings. It wasn't much, but it was real money, secret money that, at the end of the day, after doing the sums on his calculator, S handed me in an envelope.

The calculator was blue, like eye shadow.

XXIV

By S's side, I learned that vanity is good business, and I encountered the multiverse theory for the first time. For S had a parallel life with another wife and son. This other son was the same age as the one he had with the wife I knew.

We were sipping coffee when S received a telegram from someone who knew him well enough to put the coffeehouse as the address.

Sonofafuckingbitch, S said, and then he explained that before arriving at the town where we were headed that afternoon, we would have to make two stops.

The first was at a perfumery we'd already visited, where S asked them to pay an invoice in advance, before the eye shadows, lipsticks, and hair gels were delivered to their respective shelves. On S's request, I acted with greater drama than usual, and I even pretended to faint when S mentioned his sister, my supposedly bedridden mother.

The sorrow is dizzying, he said, lifting me to my feet and counting the notes.

Second stop: we pulled up outside a house. S reached for the envelope containing the money and slipped it into his pocket.

"Wait here," he said.

A woman opened the door, S went inside, and, soon after, a miniature S peeped out the window.

We looked at each other and waved.

There were two possibilities: either the door that S had stepped through was a passage to the past, and in that case the boy looking at me through the window was S forty years earlier; or, S had a child who was none of the children I knew (those children went to my school).

A while later, a small hand rapped on the door of the Citroneta and offered me a glass of juice.

When I gave him back the empty glass, the boy peeped through the car window, leaned half his body through it, and gave me a hug.

For as long as the hug lasted, I pretended to be the sister he would never meet. I pretended, the boy pretended, S was pretending; the world was a ridiculous theatre.

I watched him go back to his house and knew at that moment that sometimes it's best to let things lie. So, when S came out and shut the front door with a bang, which was followed by a vase being hurled from inside the house, he got into the car and was met with my most perfect silence.

The silence was so conspicuous that when we pulled into a petrol station, after filling the tank, S went inside and bought me an ice cream.

I decided to place what I'd seen in the category of "Things I Maybe Imagined" and, since I couldn't keep quiet forever, as a topic of conversation I brought up a game I'd learned in math class that was perfectly designed for talking without saying anything.

"Think of a number from 1 to 9 and multiply it by 9."

"Done."

"Now add up the two digits, subtract 5, and think of the letter it corresponds to in the alphabet."

"What?" (S had no patience, but he kept playing because he was afraid I would go quiet again.)

"Well if the number is 1 it's A, if it's 2, then B, if it's 3, then C…"

"Got it."

"Do you have the letter?"

"Yes."

"Now think of a country that begins with that letter."

"Okay."

"And with the second letter of that country, think of an animal."

"Is there much to go?"

"This is the last bit. Have you thought of an animal?"

"Yes."

"But there are no elephants in Denmark."

"How the fuck did you do that?"

Any number from 1 to 9 multiplied by 9 gives two digits that, when added together, are 9. On subtracting 5, that number will always be 4, which corresponds, in alphabetical order, to the letter D. And, when thinking about a country that starts with the letter D, 99 percent of human beings think of Denmark, and 97 percent, on focusing on an animal starting with E, think of an elephant. The margin of error is very small.

But instead of saying that to S, I said, "I guessed it."

"In that case, guess whether they'll buy something from us in the next store."

"They won't buy anything."

"Well then, we're finished for the day," said S, at the same time as he did a U-turn in the middle of the road.

"Let's go eat till we pop," he concluded.

So we parked in the town square and headed for a coffeehouse, where we asked for two coffees: a regular (mine), and a half serve (S's).

S filled the remainder with whisky from a flask he always carried in his pocket. It was a habit the waiters knew about (S had been visiting the same coffeehouses for twenty years) and which they no longer remarked upon because, from what I observed in those years, waiters, same as traveling salesmen, pick their battles carefully.

"To help me deal with the misadjustments, do you get me, M?"

"Gotcha."

To celebrate this communion between two human beings, something that didn't happen every day, we rounded out our coffees with four slabs of thousand layer cake, which we finished right when D showed up to collect me.

XXV

On the drives home I didn't only experience revelations about the workings of life. I also jotted down stories and messages on the notepad I kept inside my carry case.

In fact, the notepad included something like an early will and testament on the page that followed the lists of "Quid Pro Quos" and "Money" (this last one written in a code that substituted vowels for numbers).

My will was called "The Future." In it I divided my worldly goods among the people I knew. It was full of blots because, as my feelings for those individuals waxed or waned, I switched around what they would inherit. The modifications were made every day and basically depended on who I'd shared the past few hours with.

If I'd spent the afternoon with D, when night came, I bequeathed him my Kermit the Frog brooch and 150 pesos.

If, on the other hand, I'd spent the previous hours with S, I added to his list—which already included pliers, brand-name Kramp—50 pesos, and the same brooch that, meanwhile, I erased from D's list, as well as subtracting 50 pesos.

I had lists for my mother, the photographer, and a few others.

My feelings were fickle and shifting. But I didn't care about that; what I really cared about was the work that went into rewriting, erasing, and rewriting my will each night. So, in an effort to save myself some toil, I asked D when the future would arrive.

"Tomorrow morning," he responded.

And, since he looked so sure, I made the most of the situation and asked what the future was, exactly.

"Tomorrow morning," he responded once more.

XXVI

During the school break my mother granted me permission to accompany D for a whole week, which was to say that I accompanied him without having to resort to the false excuse slips or other lies about my day.

("Did you learn a lot of things at school?"

"Lots, Mamá.")

And I waited for that week to arrive, like the other kids I knew waited for Christmas, because I would be allowed to stay at a hotel overnight, just like the older salesmen.

I shared a room with D, which had its upside: I could listen to the radio as long as I wanted; and its downside: I had to wrap my head in a scarf so as not to hear his snores. This method was relatively effective; my head was small, and the scarf was long.

When I mentioned my problem to the hotel manager the next morning, she told me to imagine I was in a forest where, from a certain hour, sleeping in the bed opposite mine wasn't D but a small bear. I would cease to notice the snores and would fall asleep.

A big bear, I corrected her.

From then on, my school break was doubly productive. We would leave early to sell Kramp products; some afternoons I would accompany S; and, in the evenings, I would venture deep into the forest in my room to take care of the bear.

Everything was going well until the afternoon it rained.

Important metaphor

112

"From every which way," S would say later.

It rained, but, like stubborn fish, we visited one client, then another, and another.

I refused to take off my dripping-wet hat (I knew that the power of my character, the daughter of S's bedridden sister, resided in that hat).

When I got back, I didn't feel like dinner, and I dreamed about a tree that bloomed with nuts and door viewers. There were also glass flowers. And in the dream, I thought that such a garden wouldn't survive the winter. So, I took a saw from my pocket and cut off a piece of root. The root, once separated from the tree, turned into a piece of string, which I tied to my wrist.

The next morning, I woke with a 40-degree fever. I cried out for my mother and confused D with a real bear.

Frightened, D went downstairs to fetch some aspirin and a mug of tea with a squeeze of lemon.

He also dampened one of his white handkerchiefs with cold water and pressed it to my forehead.

I dozed all morning, and, along the blurry line that connects reality to dreams, I saw D walking from the room to the bathroom and back again, cooling the handkerchief.

"This method is fail-safe," he said, nervous, pressing the handkerchief to my forehead once more.

When he went downstairs to the dining room, he informed everybody of my feverish state. The most distressed was S, who, on remembering my wet hat the afternoon before, said again:

"The rain was coming from every which way. And she wouldn't take off the fucking hat."

For lunch I only had a bowl of chicken broth that the hotel manager brought to my room, as well as a second mug of tea, taken with a squeeze of lemon, and a comic book, which I didn't read but instead tucked beneath my pillow.

By the afternoon I felt better, but since I still couldn't get out of bed, with everybody else's permission D borrowed the only television in the hotel, and we watched a Mexican film.

I'm not sure if it was the last vestiges of the fever, but something made me ask him:

"Will I sell Kramp products forever?"

"Forever is a very long day," responded D.

And since I liked the sound of that phrase, I jotted it down on a napkin while he told me about a new Kramp product: a waterproof flashlight with a lifetime guarantee, to light up "the darkest corners."

Five minutes later, there was a knock at the door. S came in, lit a cigarette, and took a black doll out of his pocket.

"She's African, so you'd better not let her get cold," he said.

And from the same pocket he extracted a flask of whisky, which he gave to D—I'm not sure if out of paternal solidarity or guilt. S, as well as foul-mouthed, was very Catholic.

I had almost recovered by dinnertime, but out of consideration for how bad my day had been, the salesmen who were staying at the hotel didn't demand the television back, nor did they get drunk. And they went to bed on tiptoe, like well-behaved bears.

XXVII

I got over my cold—or pneumonia—but my appearance wasn't the best. I was very skinny, and two shadows—each the shape of a half-moon—settled beneath my eyes, never to fade away.

I had a recurring dream: we were traveling along the highway, and the salesmen's Renaults were flashing their headlights in different combinations. My task was to discover what they meant. Two blinks: Continue? Just one blink: Caution? Three blinks: Stop? As hard as I thought and as much as I jotted down ideas on my notepad, I didn't manage to decipher them. I woke from the dream distressed and had trouble getting back to sleep.

I returned to school and kept accompanying D, who, out of consideration for the fact that I still bore signs of convalescence, decided I wouldn't be doing double shifts anymore. S, guilty as he was, accepted this dissolution of our partnership without protest.

When D told me, I didn't feel sadness, only emptiness. Emptiness in the shape of an envelope full of cash.

Was everything that happened next D's fault? Something inside me still refuses to answer that question.

I prefer to blame E.

XXVIII

E was a secondary character in our lives. And we were secondary characters in a larger story. A series of elements—ghosts, faith in the Great Carpenter, my early vocation, the times we were living in— could have crossed paths and then continued on their way, but instead they collided head-on.

It all unfolded like this:

Our work hours were strict, and at nine in the evening we had to be indoors, preferably at home. That day we'd come home at six o'clock.

The telephone sounded. It was E. He needed D to go pick him up, and he needed me to go with

D. He had found the ghosts, he had photographed them, and this time it was more important than ever that he make it back to the city without raising any suspicions.

The basic argument—which nobody said, but we all understood—was roughly the same one S had used, so I will fall back on his language: pulling over one sonofabitch is not the same as pulling over two sonsofbitches who have a young girl in the back seat.

D's code of honor could, in exceptional cases, be extended to individuals outside the family of traveling salesmen. So, considering that E let him into the cinema free of charge whenever D wanted, and making the most of the fact that my mother wasn't home yet, he decided we would help him. It was seven o'clock. The town was an hour's drive away. At nine o'clock on the dot we would be back.

I would like to recall that, on that trip specifically, we talked about something important as we headed down the highway, but I don't.

We arrived, and E was waiting for us.

When I greeted him, I asked if he'd found the ghosts, but he didn't say anything, only took my hand and squeezed it a moment.

D looked at his watch and suggested that E lie down on the back seat, so I got into the passenger seat once more.

We were leaving the town when a car blocked our way. Two men got out.

We didn't try to hide E, as it would have been impossible. Nor did I try any of my theatrical ploys, because the little experience I had was enough for me to know that, this time, I was in the middle of a real drama.

Placing my trust in our talent—and in the theory of compassion—would have been ingenuous, so the best I could do, and what I did, was stay still in my seat.

D and E got out of the car and moved away, escorted by the two men.

Minutes went by without them returning, so I got out of the Renault and went back to the town square.

The town seemed like a desert, so I sat beneath a tree—a mulberry—and pulled a cigarette out of my bag.

The smoke rings rose and, on watching them dissipate, I had the second epiphany of my life. I shrank and was borne away on one of my smoke rings.

On that privileged night journey I saw how the stars amassed heat and: POOF! appeared. Millenia went by, they consumed their last reserves of hydrogen, and POOF! they dissolved.

The view of the stars blended with that of

the tacks, which, even though they were made of stainless steel, didn't escape the cycle of dissolution (POOF! POOF! POOF! POOF!).

Swinging from my smoke ring, I got a privileged view of things.

And it was while I was experiencing this clarity of mind that I heard a hoarse voice shout:

"Let's see if you'll still feel like digging up bones when you're in hell, you fucking dog."

Why the word "privileged"?

XXIX

The bullets that were fired a few seconds later ripped open one, two, three, four, five black holes. And through one of those black holes passed a "lucky beetle."[2]

---

2 "Lucky beetles" are not a species, but an insect that alights in the exact spot where life took a different course. That spacetime in which one chooses to walk down one side of the road or the other, to leave the house or not, to say or to refrain from saying something. It's a fraction of a second so small that only an insect can pass through it. An insect that, when it appears, parts life in two.

XXX

The next morning, I was found unconscious beneath the tree in the town square, with the onset of hypothermia. I was taken to a store and given something to drink—alcohol, I imagine—which revived me enough that I could say my phone number and my mother's name.

THE CALL AND THE CONVERSATION THAT CAME NEXT

When my mother got the call, the part of her that had been absent for so many years came back in a flash. What she didn't know was that this happened the day after E had found, buried among the others, the ghost that had kept her asleep to us for so long.

I found this out years later when, looking for a backpack, I came across a box with photographs and clippings from newspapers about the discovery of several bodies.

All towns are alike, but it didn't take me too much of an effort to recognize the town in the image as the town of the gunshots.

Had E made more calls? Had he sent a smoke signal that said *I've found them*?

I will never know; nor is it important.

What is important is the interrogation that came after.

Because I told my mother about the ghost town, E's call, the gunshots.

And about S and the envelopes too. About the booklet of false excuse slips. About the hardware stores, perfumeries, S's little double, skipping school, and, finally, the Great Carpenter.

As I went on with my story, I'm not sure why, but I started crying, and once I'd started, I cried for several hours. My mother held me close and said that everything would be alright in a voice I didn't recognize.

At the same time, another interrogation was happening. The one endured by D.

I will never know what D said. What my mother knew was that D would be back. He was wily enough to convince his interrogators. And cowardly enough not to risk going down in history as a heroic ghost. He would be freed. And he could go to hell.

XXXI

When D came home several kilos lighter with a three-day beard and bruises all over his body, my mother and I had left for what I called our "next life."

Before we left, my mother placed on the table a note containing two words, one that she'd learned from my grandmother, and another from her own repertoire: "foolish bastard."

Right beside it, I left an envelope with the money I'd saved over the course of my remunerated employment, and a letter that said:

"I love you.

P.S. This is a loan."

XXXII

We traveled all night in a bus that took my mother and me far enough away.

Far from D.

Far from Kramp products.

Far from ghosts.

And the list of things that were now distant affected me profoundly. So much so that on two occasions I tried to take my life by holding my breath. I failed and, at nine years of age, understood that the self-preservation instinct really was something else.

I explained this to two of my new classmates with those two words: "something else." And then I urged them to eliminate themselves; they only had to concentrate and stop breathing.

I didn't want them to die, I just want to verify that what had faltered in me wasn't my own determination (which was all that was needed to stop breathing), but that of the entire human race. And I verified it because they, like me, survived.

My mother was called, and she asked my teacher, in front of me, to please forgive me, that I was going through a rough patch because of a family breakdown.

I could have explained to my mother and my new teacher that breakdowns of other kinds could be added to the family one: a spiritual breakdown (when I spoke to him from this new city, the Great Carpenter couldn't hear me); a financial breakdown (I no longer had quid pro quos or envelopes);

a vocational breakdown (I was a traveling salesman assistant, and in this new city there were no traveling salesmen).

Trauma, uprootedness

Would they have understood?

Not likely, so I didn't say anything.

I decided to let life run its course and it did so with such ease that the following year I had a new father, was soon to have a sister, and we even bought a dog.

"Flaco," that's what we named the dog.

XXXIII

I went to school, played with my sister, walked Flaco, and even had time to make new friends.

It was true that sometimes my gaze would rest on some door viewer or cheap cologne, and I would feel a slight disquiet. But just like a Buddhist monk—a friend of my mother's, also new, had said as much—I let those thoughts go.

Twice a year I got a call from D.

"How are you, M?"

"Good."

"How's the new city?"

"Horrible."

"I couldn't call you; did you see the news about the telephone thief?"

"No."

"He didn't leave a single one. We were incommunicado for several months."

(Silence.)

"I'll try to come visit someday. Sales are down. People have so many screws loose that the floor is littered with them, so they don't need to buy them at hardware stores."

(Laughter.)

"Take care, M."

"You too. Goodbye."

We never said *I miss you*. And we didn't talk about what had happened, either.

It was better that way.

What's
Said and
not said

XXXIV

The ensuing years went by in slow motion. They were so similar that they could have been concentrated into a single day. To help me perceive the passing of time, at the beginning of each year I bought a calendar. I hung it on the wall, crossed off the days, and, when the calendars ended, stowed them in a box I kept beneath the bed.

In that box was the photo that E had taken of me, and my sales notepad, too.

What I was safekeeping there was a time machine.

One.

Two.

Three.

Four.

Plus a year when I had no calendar, but that also counted: five years went by.

And I decided enough time had passed, so I sat down to wait for the next call.

The telephone sounded when summer number six was beginning.

"How are you, M?"

"I'm coming to see you."

(Silence.)

"In one month exactly, wait for me at the train station coffeehouse."

"I'll be there."

"Remember, you owe me money."

"I remember."

For the past five years, I'd been walking the neighbor's dog, too. The neighbor was a confirmed bachelor who, for someone as bitter as he, paid very well. If I added the money D owed me to those savings, I calculated that I had enough to get by for a month in one of the hotels.

I had no trouble obtaining permission to travel. My mother, influenced by my new father, now believed in Buddha, but that didn't mean she had stopped admiring independence movements. So she lent me her backpack and entrusted me to the primordial emptiness.

MY MOTHER'S BACKPACK

The pieces missing from the puzzle that was my mother were there, inside her backpack. A backpack from the time before I came into existence, before D appeared in her life. Inside it she had placed a bundle of letters, three books, and a blue handkerchief with white spots.

Jaime Andrés Suárez Moncada had given her those things.

María José Ferrada

And, after giving them to her, Jaime Andrés Suárez Moncada had disappeared.

When she found out, my mother took up a needle and thread and started to embroider a star on her backpack, thinking that when she finished it, Jaime Andrés Suárez Moncada would appear in the doorway of her house and kiss her. But that never happened.

For years after, she searched for Jaime Andrés Suárez Moncada. But all she found were lists of names.

She tucked them into the outer pocket of her backpack.

The backpack was heavy, and my mother, who insisted on wearing it, became more stooped with each passing day.

The world of ghosts is as small as the world of humans.

Years later, the remains of Jaime Andrés Suárez Moncada were found by the man who had been his best friend: E, the photographer.

HOW TO ORDER THE UNIVERSE

News of the fact appeared in a newspaper that seemed to be from another country, a newspaper that someone had forwarded to my mother inside an envelope that had no sender's address.

The body of her first love, Jaime Andrés Suárez Moncada, was peppered with thirteen black holes and had several broken bones.

Why was he killed?

When my mother finished reading, she shut herself in the bathroom with a needle (the same one she had used to embroider the star on the backpack) and a bottle of black ink.

She made thirteen punctures on her arm because she wanted her body to feel pain on the outside like it was feeling on the inside. She pricked herself thirteen times. Hard, really hard.

Later, when I asked her what those moles were, she said she didn't know. That she had simply woken that morning with a black constellation on her left arm.

My mother comes out with the weirdest things, I thought.

My mother, who had been crying again.

XXXV

Exactly one month after our phone call, D was waiting for me on the platform.

Instead of embracing, we gave each other slaps on the back, as old school friends do.

The same suit.

The same sample case.

But, of course, no more Renault.

So, we took a bus, which deposited us at D's new house—a tidy, tiny attic. To me it seemed so perfect that I thought of a clock. A clock that made irregular revolutions. In that place, preparing a welcome coffee for me, D seemed like a human being whom time had left inside some kind of parenthesis.

And it was so nice, cheating time, that by mid-day I had already set up some of my things on the desk and was measuring the couch to see if my fourteen-year-old body would fit on it.

"Just for a week," said D.

"I have money for a whole month, and I'm thinking that if I stay here on the couch, that will save me what I'd spend on a hotel."

"Two weeks, not a day more."

"In that case, I'll take the bed and you can take the couch."

For the next few days we tried to resume our old routine.

Since we didn't have the Renault, we made the trips by bus or train. It was at one of the stations that, on being up close to other people, I noticed that there was something strange about us.

From one moment to the next, well-shined shoes, which had been symbolic of a belief—the possibility of walking on the moon—had become a tactic to draw attention away from D's worn-out shirt. The same went for my T-shirt, which I myself had chosen for the occasion, and the kerchief that I had tied around my neck.

There were two possibilities:

A. Precariousness had always been with us, and I'd never noticed.

B. Something had changed.

Whichever it was, my childhood memories fractured: crack. And I hated the Great Carpenter, not for the reality but for the insight, which enveloped me in an unpleasant—and until now unknown—shame whenever I felt the gaze of others upon us. Did they know? Did they see our precariousness?

For the first time I saw them clearly, and it seemed to me that they were giants.

And it was thinking on this scale, and seeing our disadvantage, that, after years of boring reality, gave me a new vision: D and I were vanishing.

The people on the platform waited, said good-bye, or went to look for their cars.

D and I, in contrast, kept still, and at first started to lose our colors, then our shapes. We became smoke rings. And we disintegrated as we crossed the sky above the city.

There, abandoned on the platform, only his sample case and my backpack remained.

Years went by. Hundreds of years. It was the same spot, but the landscape had changed: where before there was the station and the city, now there was a desert crowded with containers.

Our things were still there, and the inhabitants lay wreaths of paper before them.

We had existed a long time earlier and, contrary to what I had imagined, disappearance itself wasn't painful at all.

You turn into smoke. People of the future do what they can with your remains.

I had understood one of the workings of existence. And I would have gone even further if D hadn't told me our train was waiting.

In a few hours, we arrived at our destination.

We made our first stop at a coffeehouse. No traveling salesman showed up to keep us company, so we quickly set off for the leading hardware store.

This newfound solitude was repeated over the next few days. It made the image of the desert materialize again and settle on the coffees I ordered. I stirred the image with my teaspoon, dispersing it.

XXXVI

We kept on: every day, a town. But something in the landscape we moved through didn't match the snapshot of reality I'd filed in my head.

At first, I went inside the hardware stores with D, but it turned out my body was too big to play my old part. The centimeters that my arms and legs had gained in the past few years had made me invisible to those in charge.

I cursed the Great Carpenter again. If He could keep dwarfs and ponies small, He could have done so with me. But He hadn't, and His decision had left me at a loss.

I had to have a think. So, instead of accompanying D, I decided I would wait for him outside.

When I asked him for the Kramp catalogue to bring myself up to date, he said they didn't print them anymore. The little he sold, he sold from memory. That's what he said.

Financial pinch

I realized the situation was more critical than I had imagined, and, if I didn't want the ground to disappear beneath my feet, it would be best to bring my trip to an end.

I still had a few memories in my head that hadn't blended with this new reality, and I wanted to preserve them. So, I said goodbye to D, and gave him more slaps on the back, a hug, and a kiss.

I had a week left, and some money, so I decided to call S.

XXXVII

He came to collect me at the coffeehouse where I said I'd be waiting, tooting the horn from a block away. My happiness to see him was so great that I ran out without paying for the coffees I'd had while I waited.

"You got big! You're of no use now, but it's wonderful to see you again."

He hugged me tightly, and I breathed in the unmistakable smell of alcohol and cheap cologne that I'd kept safe for so long in my store of fond memories.

"I found out you've been going hungry the past few years, so I brought you a cheese sandwich. I prepared it myself."

I could still recognize the food sold along the highway. On confirming that S was as deceitful as ever and the bread was as dry as I remembered, I recovered some of the territory lost.

To celebrate our reunion, he opened the glove box: the flask of liquor was there, just like old times.

He offered me a sip, which I accepted with thanks. The whisky burned my throat, but it was good. It was when I placed the flask back in the glove box that I saw the revolver. I'd never held one in my hands, so I grasped it carefully.

"Poof!" yelled S.

Don't be a moron, you don't joke around with a loaded weapon. I would have liked to yell that at him, but even though several years had passed, I still felt something like respect for S.

"Why do you have that here?"

"To kill myself."

"I'm serious."

"So am I. You leave it there; I want to be the one to decide when my time comes."

He explained that business wasn't good. The sonsofbitches of the big chains, those fuckers, were eating up small and midsized businesses. And as soon as they were done smacking their lips after polishing off hardware stores, perfumeries, pharmacies, and clothing stores, nobody would have any need for traveling salesmen.

That's why he had decided to buy a truckload of revolvers. Because he bought the whole load, the gun-store owner—an ex-policeman—had given him a good price. All the traveling salesmen would pull the trigger in unison the day the last business closed.

"Does D have one too?'

"We all do."

I could have told him he was nuts. That all of them were absolutely nuts. But instead I said:

"I understand."

For the next few days we continued southward, staying in hotels that were so uncomfortable we might as well have slept out in the open.

With scarcity on all fronts urging us on (or, rather, thanks to it), we managed to perform a bad rendition of our old operation. I sat quietly in the car, and S explained to the perfumery owners that the silhouette they could make out in the distance was that of his quadriplegic niece, who was now his responsibility.

"Do you remember the Turk?" he said to me as we passed by his store.

"The man with the three-day sales."

"That's the one."

"What happened to him?"

"He hired a secretary who only allowed one-hour visits. You think it's possible to fill a fucking freight wagon that quickly?"

"No."

"That's why we stopped selling to the Turkish fag."

The week came to an end, so I said goodbye to S with another hug. From the station, I watched him walk away until he became a blurred speck, like an image that you keep inside your head but can't quite bring into focus.

XXXVIII

I went home, inside me an emptiness the size of the backpack I'd borrowed from my mother. Since I needed to find a reason for the emptiness, I blamed the amount owing that I hadn't collected. I'd crossed half the country to recover it and had come back empty-handed. I was a failure. One hiding a second failure, which I still didn't know what to call.

I went back to my routine: school, dogs, my mother, my new father, my sister.

The others. In a couple of weeks, they'd grown a few centimeters and I'd shrunk a few. They didn't seem to notice, but I did. And in those brief moments of awareness, the only solution was to make the most of any excuse to hug my sister or my mother.

I didn't want to disappear. And to stop that from happening, I had to cling to Planet Earth.

XXXIX

Months went by, and the black hole was still there. I decided to cover it up by busying myself with being a good person. And the truth was, at that very moment, the bad people I loved so much could have been blowing their brains out, a clear sign that, if I wanted to survive, I had to switch sides.

I worked on bettering my grades and my manners, spent more time with my sister, and even told jokes during family lunches. Perfect.

The next thing would be to make a doghouse. I would buy the materials myself.

María José Ferrada

Is it good to know the inner workings of things? To know what makes them tick?

I still don't have an answer for that. I only know that when I went to the hardware store and asked for twenty twelve-millimeter nails and a hammer, brand-name Kramp, the shop assistant told me they hadn't stocked them for years. The company had closed its local branch three or four years before; she couldn't remember when exactly.

She started to list other brands, which I listened to as one listens to a far-off murmur. The rumbling of the sea, that's what I thought of, and I asked her to sell me a couple of planks. If I could feel their weight, if I could hold them in my hands and take them home, it meant I was still a real person.

I walked home, and I have a distinct memory of how, on the way, the afternoon breeze kept messing up a length of my hair that fell across the left side of my forehead. I pushed it back in place a couple of times, and then I let it be.

When I arrived, I went straight to the rear patio. I left the planks on the ground and, leaning my back against the rear wall, sat down to gaze at the space between me and the house. How much breeze had blown across there? For how many millions of years had that space existed?

When finally I went inside, I told my mother I wasn't hungry and went straight to my room.

XL

Just a few months earlier, I'd been with D, trying to sell products that no longer existed, which was the equivalent of saying that D had lied to me.

What I felt wasn't anger.

I remembered him saying, so many times, that it was improbable that a house constructed from 80 percent Kramp products would collapse in the event of an earthquake or a tornado, and realized that mine was one of the unfortunate cases that fell within the improbability.

For the earthquake had come, the feared tornado, and my construction, made from 95 percent Kramp products, was now a pile of sticks.

María José Ferrada

What I felt wasn't anger, but an emptiness that turned into a black hole. One that fit perfectly inside my other black hole, the one I'd carried within me since visiting D without knowing why. Now I knew.

I sat down to wait for the next call. I knew D was very organized and that, come December, he would look at his diary and see the note he'd jotted down at the beginning of the year: Call M.

On December 1st, at seven o'clock in the evening, the telephone sounded.

I was too tired to be original, so I repeated the same words from the time before. I would be there, in one month exactly, at the station.

D responded, with a similar weariness, that he would be waiting.

XLI

I stuffed only a few items of clothing into the backpack. It was summer, and something within me knew this would be a short trip.

When I got off the train, I saw D at the station and noted that, despite the heat, he was wearing winter clothing.

We went to his house to have some coffee.

I wanted to ask him why he'd said nothing about Kramp products disappearing, nothing about the pistol he'd bought, and nothing about the money he owed me.

But instead I lit a cigarette and said the coffee was excellent.

As if something was urging us on, before midday we took a bus southward and stepped off it in the first town we came to.

I told D that this time I wouldn't go with him into the hardware store, that I had come solely to keep him company and would wait for him in the town square. I had brought a book with me: *Gulliver's Travels*.

D went off with his sample case to try to sell his nonexistent products. Seen from a distance, the hardware store looked unreal to me too.

Half an hour later he came back and sat down beside me.

"How did you go?"

"I sold two-hundred door viewers and collected the amount owing for ninety saws."

We were silent for a bit. And that was when I saw the mulberry tree and realized we were in the same town square where I'd collapsed from fear years before.

We lit a cigarette, and then another.

For hours that seemed like years, D and I stayed seated, silent.

"Keep it."

"Keep what."

"The money."

And when I finished speaking, I understood I was telling him goodbye.

We had been deeply united by a catalogue of hardware store products: nails, hammers, door viewers, screws. But that catalogue no longer existed.

Everything kept on according to inner workings that we couldn't stop.

We saw the first star of the night.

Billions of years before, on that same night, the big bang had taken place, and from then on everything drew apart, and continued to draw apart, irretrievably.

María José Ferrada

Up there, the waning moon was the same one that Neil Armstrong had walked on years before. But other things had changed forever.

My father left me at the station where I'd arrived the same morning. And we said goodbye knowing we would never see each other again.

Surprisingly, the train pulled away on time.

I rested my head on the window.

I fell asleep.

M's way of understanding the world keeps changing while those of adults stay the same and atrophy

READER'S GUIDE

1. Why do you think María José Ferrada wanted to tell this story from M's precocious, though limited, perspective? If you could read this book from another character's point of view, how would the story be different?

2. Why do you think the characters are only referred to by their initials?

3. Early on, M says that "my parents designed a learning plan that would allow me to comprehend the things that a child—a girl, in this case—needed in order to make her way in the world. Thus, I began early with a classification of things." How does M's relentless categorization of objects and the people around her help her cope with the changing world and challenges she is faced with?

4. How does the photographer, E, change the dynamic of the father/daughter relationship?

5. Much of the book's prose is rooted in metaphor, such as D's motto that "every life has its own moon landing." What does he mean by this, and how does it relate to his own life as a traveling salesman?

6. Augusto Pinochet's dictatorship looms in the background of the novel; how does it inform the everyday lives of the characters in the book?

7. Throughout the story, M's mother is an "off-screen" character. Why do you think the author makes this choice?

8. M says she thinks of her excursions with her father as "an extension" of her schooling. What does she learn with him that she might not in school? Outside of school, where do you feel you learned the most valuable life lessons?

9. At one point in the book, salesmen share tall tales that get more outlandish with each retelling. In what ways do they, and M, mythologize their work, and how does it compare to reality?

10. Are there other narrators that M reminds you of? What are some of your favorite books narrated by younger voices?

MARÍA JOSÉ FERRADA's children's books have been published all over the world. *How to Order the Universe* has been or is being translated into Italian, Brazilian Portuguese, Danish, and German, and is also being published all over the Spanish-speaking world. Ferrada has been awarded numerous prizes, such as the City of Orihuela de Poesía, Premio Hispanoamericano de Poesía para Niños, the Academia Award for the best book published in Chile, and the Santiago Municipal Literature Award, and is a three-time winner of the Chilean Ministry of Culture Award. She lives in Santiago, Chile.

ELIZABETH BRYER is a translator and writer from Australia. Her translations include Claudia Salazar Jiménez's Americas Prize–winning *Blood of the Dawn*; Aleksandra Lun's *The Palimpsests*, for which she was awarded a PEN/Heim Translation Fund grant; and José Luis de Juan's *Napoleon's Beekeeper*. Her debut novel, *From Here On, Monsters*, is out now through Picador.